KU-168-713

JigSaw

A PUZZLE IN THE POST

WALKER BOOKS
AND SUBSIDIARIES
LONDON · BOSTON · SYDNEY · AUCKLAND

First published 2022 by Walker Books Ltd
87 Vauxhall Walk, London SE11 5HJ

10 9 8 7 6 5 4 3 2 1

© 2022 Blackbird Design Pty Ltd

The right of Bob Graham to be identified as the author and
illustrator of this work has been asserted in accordance with the
Copyright, Designs and Patents Act 1988

This book has been typeset in ITC Usherwood

Printed in China

All rights reserved. No part of this book may be reproduced,
transmitted or stored in an information retrieval system in
any form or by any means, graphic, electronic or mechanical,
including photocopying, taping and recording, without prior
written permission from the publisher.

British Library Cataloguing in Publication Data:
a catalogue record for this book is available from the British
Library

ISBN 978-1-5295-0331-9

www.walker.co.uk

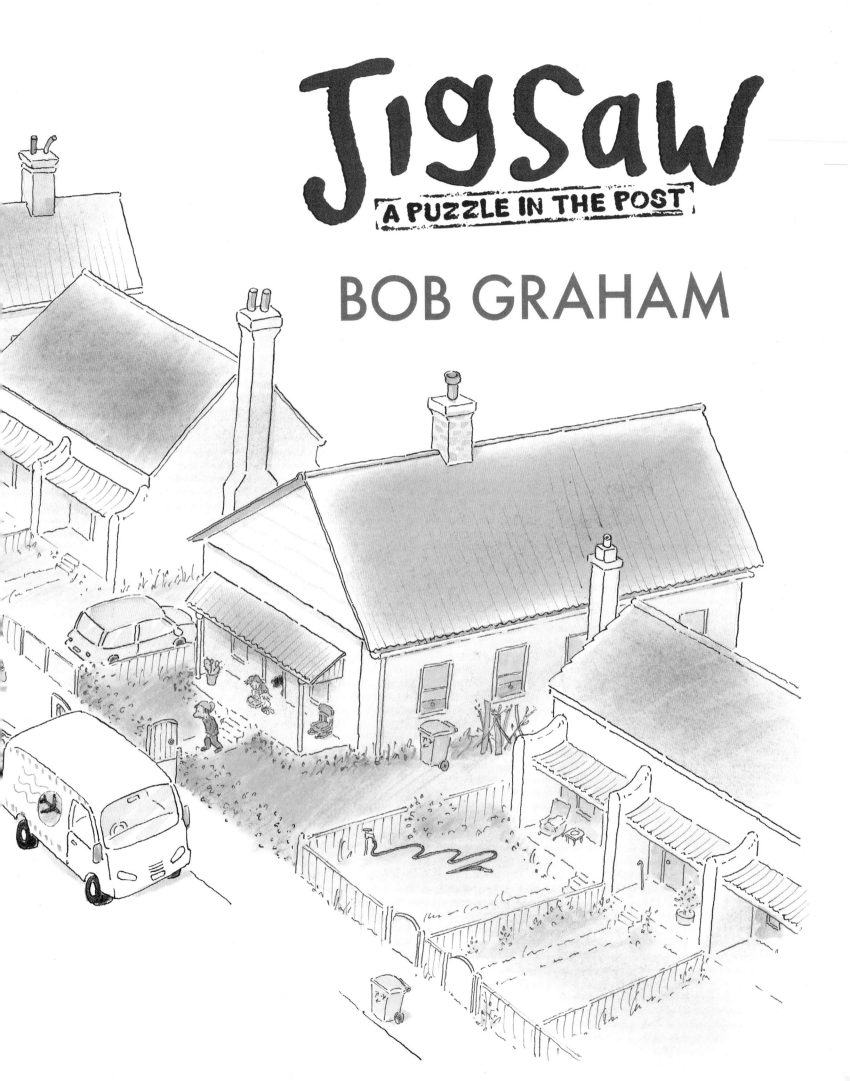

Jigsaw
A PUZZLE IN THE POST

BOB GRAHAM

No one knew just who it was sent by.

It arrived one day all covered with stamps.

A beautiful jigsaw – an African sunrise.

"Good luck to you all" was all the card said.

The Kellys stood there and undid the wrapping.

"Oh! Let's do it!" said Kitty and Katie and Mum.

"I've got time on my hands…" said Dad,

and set his watch to Late Autumn.

"Let's get started," said the Kellys.

Early in Winter they completed the edges.

Kitty

and Katie,

and Lucy helped too.

The girls went out playing in Spring and in Summer,
but Dad kept his head down just getting it done.
With Autumn approaching they sorted the colours –
as a beautiful dawn began to emerge.
"The hippo's swim shorts…" said Dad.

They looked high and low. They looked under Kitty.

They looked under Lucy and everywhere else.

Then Mum stopped and she thought.

Yes she did some hard thinking...

"I think I've got it!" said Mum.

"Where is it?" they said.

"Went out in the rubbish?" she whispered.

"We'll find it," Dad said,
"if it takes us all Autumn."
"Oh! Let's do it," said Kitty
and Katie and Mum.

Dad looked at his watch,
and the leaves started falling.

"Jigsaw piece missing; Hippo's swim shorts," Dad said,
and the man stroked his chin. "Yes! People come looking,
but they don't often find them. Try the stack at the end."

"Some hope's what we need, to see things a bit clearer."

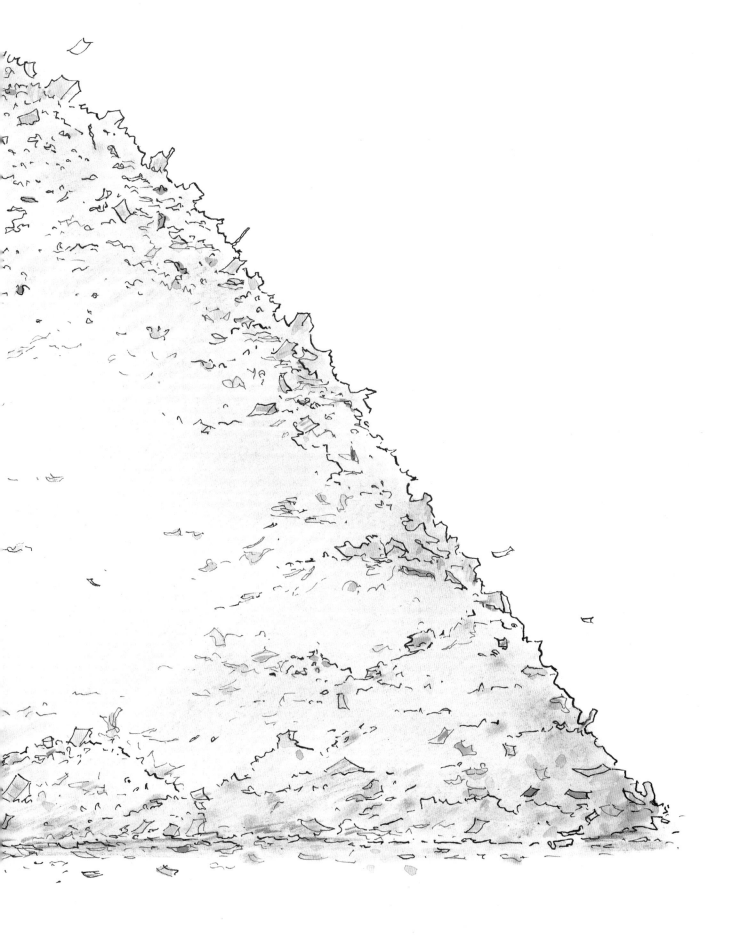

"Let's start here, then," said Katie. "Shouldn't take long."

There were letters of love from faraway places, letters of sorrow, notes of forgiveness, bus tickets, train tickets, cards saying "thank you", and newspapers old and forgotten in time.

Old confetti from weddings, a sock no one wanted,
a note that said, "I'll meet you at twenty to nine"
and "Sorry for your troubles" (attached to old flowers).
"Get well", said another, sealed with a kiss.

There were shopping lists – too many to mention –
an old soldier's photo yellow with age,
and every so often a breeze would lift them
and put them back down like falling rain.

They looked up, they looked down.

"Let's look at it this way, it's just

waiting around and will find us again."

"That's wishful thinking," said Mum.

"Let's wish then," said Katie …

and they sadly
went home.

Through the front door, back into the kitchen.

It was Dad's boot
that had now lost it…

It was Kitty who found it.

"Can't believe that we missed it.

Must have been there the whole time."

So with Autumn here with them
the puzzle was finished.

It was Kitty who placed it,
her sister who straightened it.

The hippo found his swim shorts,
and the sun came up out of Africa.

To whoever it was who sent them the puzzle,

Katie wrote back (with pictures by Kitty).

She addressed it to Nowear, and Mum said,

"Well, they have to live somewhere."

So Katie changed it to Sumwear.

With enough stamps to cover its travels …

and with a Hope and a Wish and a "shouldn't take long"
they went out into the Autumn twilight.

Kitty dropped it in the postbox.

A small boat on a wide ocean of letters.